The Shepherd Boy's Christmas

by Bunshu Iguchi

English text by Peggy Blakeley

Judson Press,® Valley Forge

Original edition published in Japan by
Shiko Sha Company, Ltd., Toyko, Japan, 1974

© 1976 (illustrations) Shiko Sha Company Ltd.
© 1977 (English text) A. & C. Black Ltd.

Published in the U.S.A. in 1978 by Judson Press, Valley Forge, PA 19481

Printed in Japan

ISBN 0-8170-0789-X

It was evening,
and two people were traveling along
in the sunset.
The woman rode on a donkey,
and her husband walked beside her.
They moved slowly for they had traveled
a long way and were very tired.

On the hillside the little shepherd boy
watched them go.
He had become used to strangers,
for many people had come to Bethlehem
to pay their taxes.
But he felt worried for this couple,
for he knew that in the town
all the inns and houses were full
and they would have trouble
finding a place to stay.

"I know," thought the little shepherd boy,
"They could sleep in the stable behind
our house.
It won't be as comfortable as the inn,
but it's clean and dry and warm
and better than nothing."
"I'll go quickly and tell them," he said,
and he began to run down to the town.

Back on the hillside with his sheep,
the little shepherd boy sat cross-legged by
his fire
and warmed himself.

He thought about the couple called Mary and Joseph
whom he had talked to
and helped to find a place to stay.
He knew that in some way
they were rather special people
though he didn't know why.

It was a quiet and peaceful night,
and the stars burned brightly.

All at once the sky was lit up
by the bright and shining light
of a star that shone in the east.
And on the wind came the sound of voices
singing and calling
and telling that a baby King had been
born in a stable in Bethlehem.

The little shepherd boy was frightened
but very excited, for he thought he knew
where to go to find the baby King.

And he ran down the hillside
toward the lights of the little town of Bethlehem.

He found Mary and Joseph
and the baby
in the stable
behind his father's house
and felt proud and pleased
that he had helped them.

And suddenly it was morning,
a bright and beautiful morning.

And as the little shepherd boy
guided his sheep across the pasture,
he was thankful and happy
that he'd been the first
to know about the birth of the baby King.
"Jesus is his name," he said softly to himself.
"They've called him Jesus."

Bunoku